BOOK CLUB IN A BOX

Bookclub-in-a-Box presents the discussion companion for Rohinton Mistry's novel

A Fine Balance

Published by McClelland & Stewart Inc, Toronto, 1995.
ISBN: 0-7710-6052-1

Quotations used in this guide have been taken from the text of the paperback edition of **A Fine Balance**. All information taken from other sources is acknowledged.

This discussion companion for **A Fine Balance** has been prepared and written by Marilyn Herbert, originator of Bookclub-in-a-Box. Marilyn Herbert. B.Ed., is a teacher, librarian, speaker and writer. Bookclub-in-a-Box is a unique guide to current fiction and classic literature intended for book club discussions, educational study seminars, and personal pleasure. For more information about the Bookclub-in-a-Box team, visit our website.

Bookclub-in-a-Box discussion companion for A Fine Balance

ISBN 10: 1-897082-09-6
ISBN 13: 97781897082096

This guide reflects the perspective of the Bookclub-in-a-Box team and is the sole property of Bookclub-in-a-Box.

©2005 BOOKCLUB-IN-A-BOX
©2007 2ND EDITION - AU

CONTACT INFORMATION: SEE BACK COVER.

BOOKCLUB-IN-A-BOX
Rohinton Mistry's A Fine Balance

BOOKCLUB-IN-A-BOX

Readers and Leaders Guide

Each Bookclub-in-a-Box guide is clearly and effectively organized to give you information and ideas for a lively discussion, as well as to present the major highlights of the novel. The format, with a Table of Contents, allows you to pick and choose the specific points you wish to talk about. It does not have to be used in any prescribed order. In fact, it is meant to support, not determine, your discussion.

You Choose What to Use.

You may find that some information is repeated in more than one section and may be cross-referenced so as to provide insight on the same idea from different angles.

The guide is formatted to give you extra space to make your own notes.

How to Begin

Relax and look forward to enjoying your bookclub.

With Bookclub-in-a-Box as your behind the scenes support, there is little for you to do in the way of preparation.

Some readers like to review the guide after reading the novel; some before. Either way, the guide is all you will need as a companion for your discussion. You may find that the guide's interpretation, information, and background have sparked other ideas not included.

Having read the novel and armed with Bookclub-in-a-Box, you will be well prepared to lead or guide or listen to the discussion at hand.

Lastly, if you need some more 'hands-on' support, feel free to contact us. (See Contact Information)

What to Look For

Each Bookclub-in-a-Box guide is divided into easy-to-use sections, which include points on characters, themes, writing style and structure, literary or historical background, author information, and other pertinent features unique to the novel being discussed. These may vary slightly from guide to guide.

INTERPRETATION OF EACH NOVEL REFLECTS THE PERSPECTIVE OF THE BOOKCLUB-IN-A-BOX TEAM.

Do We Need to Agree?
THE ANSWER TO THIS QUESTION IS NO.

If we have sparked a discussion or a debate on certain points, then we are happy. We invite you to share your group's alternative findings and experiences with us. You can respond on-line at our website or contact us through our Contact Information. We would love to hear from you.

Discussion Starters

There are as many ways to begin a bookclub discussion as there are members in your group. If you are an experienced group, you will already have your favorite ways to begin. If you are a newly formed group or a group looking for new ideas, here are some suggestions.

Ask for people's impressions of the novel. (This will give you some idea about which parts of the unit to focus on.)

- Identify a favorite or major character.
- Identify a favorite or major idea.
- Begin with a powerful or pertinent quote. (not necessarily from the novel)
- Discuss the historical information of the novel. (not applicable to all novels)
- If this author is familiar to the group, discuss the range of his/her work and where this novel stands in that range.
- Use the discussion topics and questions in the Bookclub-in-a-Box guide.

If you have further suggestions for discussion starters, be sure to share them with us and we will share them with others.

Above All, Enjoy Yourselves

INTRODUCTION

Suggested Beginnings

Novel Quickline

Keys to the Novel

Author Information

Historical Information

INTRODUCTION

Suggested Beginnings

1. Life is always a balancing act, whether it is in the extreme instances depicted by Mistry or in our own less urgent situations.

Discuss how each of the characters in this book finds balance. Why does Maneck fail at maintaining a balance of dignity, independence, and hope?

2. No one in the story remains whole; everyone is somehow maimed or dismembered. These horrors resonate on both the personal and national levels. Nearly thirty years after its partition and independence, India continued to suffer from regional, religious, and economic divisions.

What is Mistry suggesting about India's general welfare in 1975? Has the situation changed?

3. The title of Mistry's third novel, **Family Matters**, suggests one of his ongoing preoccupations, evident even in **A Fine Balance**. Dina, Maneck, Ishvar, and Om sew together a family from their disparate lives.

Compare the family unit in India in 1975 to the one in North America today.

4. The role of women is an important issue in the novel. Dina struggles to maintain her independence as a woman. Her adult life in the city is contrasted with her childhood under Nusswan's control and with the lives of many other women, some of whom are only casually mentioned in the novel.

Consider the position of strong independent women in a patriarchal society generally and in this novel specifically.

5. Everything and everyone in this novel gets recycled in some way. No scrap of tissue goes unused, whether it is salvaged for Dina's sanitary napkins, or for a quilt, or whether it is hair that is collected and resold. Body parts are commodified and recycled into the economic marketplace. People too are commodified: when they are maimed or damaged, Beggarmaster finds new uses for them as beggars.

How does the idea of recycling contribute to the setting and atmosphere in the novel? As citizens of a prosperous nation, we are used to a "disposable" culture. Discuss the cultural and value differences between our own and other societies.

More points to consider

1. Mistry uses his characters to discuss the caste system. Those higher in the caste seem removed from those beneath them and are unable to see the details and the pain of their lives.

Is this ignorance or prejudice or both?

2. Each character faces his or her destiny either by accepting it or succumbing to it.

What is Mistry saying about fate and destiny?

3. Mistry's vision of an ideally balanced family (nation) is to have power and rights shared equally by gender and caste. He uses the image of Dina, Maneck, and the tailors working in their tiny flat as a framework for this vision.

Is this vision possible in India, given the way that the social structure of the society has historically evolved?

4. Given Roopa's social status, should readers be shocked or surprised by Roopa's statement? *"My son does not sew for your kind."* (p.153)

Discuss this statement in relation to the possibility and reality of real future change.

Novel Quickline

Set in 1975 after Indira Gandhi has declared a state of emergency in India, **A Fine Balance** unites four characters, each of whom has suffered a loss. Dina Dalal's husband dies on their third wedding anniversary. In order to preserve her own independence, she takes a job as a supervisor for a clothing-export factory. The two tailors she hires, Ishvar and Omprakash, have come to the city in search of work after their homes have been destroyed. At the same time, Dina opens her home to a boarder, the young Maneck Kohlah, whose family still suffers the repercussions of having lost their lands in the 1947 partition. National politics intrude at every turn in these characters' lives, despite their own attempts to disengage themselves from all things political.

These four people, who suffer every imaginable indignity (and some unimaginable ones too), are torn and tattered remnants of human beings, yet they somehow manage to sew together the scraps of their individual lives to create a strong, supportive family. These four wonderfully vivid characters, who have been thrown together by the fortunes of fate, must make their way along the track of life with its endless twists and turns, stops and starts.

By joining their forces together instead of forging ahead alone, they are better able to balance themselves on life's journey. Their relationship transcends the constricting boundaries of class, caste, and religion.

Keys to the Novel

Social Realism

- Mistry's novel retains an air of anonymity – the prime minister and the City by the Sea both go unnamed and unidentified – but we recognize that his story is firmly grounded in a real time and place, India in the 1970s. Mistry has been quoted as saying that India is his focus *"because of the people ... their capacity for laughter, their capacity to endure ... Perhaps my main intention in writing this novel was to look at history from the bottom up."* **(Nunez)** The story that Mistry tells examines the lives of the lower classes; it is not a study of those in power. However, the story begins with the political decisions that affect the people of the lower castes. Mistry doesn't gloss over the negative parts of this specific time in Indian history.

Boundaries

- **A Fine Balance** depicts a traditional society plagued by poverty and a strict caste system. Yet its cast of characters continually crosses all kinds of boundaries. Ishvar and Om cross caste boundaries by taking up tailoring, while Dina crosses gender boundaries by declining the traditional role of housewife and taking on the responsibilities of both breadwinner and bread maker. Together with Maneck, these disparate people form a family that defies the conventional notion of an Indian family. The ability of these characters to oppose the norm illustrates a kind of resilience that can only be built as a result of determination and hardship, yet their situations remain hard and vulnerable.
  - Dina surrenders her independence and moves in with her brother's family.
  - Om and Ishvar are forced to become beggars.
  - Maneck distances himself from his former "family."

Author Background

Rohinton Mistry was born in Bombay (now known as Mumbai) in 1952, into a Parsi family in a small community committed to Zoroastrianism. His ancestors, like those of the other members in this community, had fled Iran (then Persia) in the eighth century to escape Islamic persecution. As a young man, he was involved in sports, and cricket in particular. He taught himself to play the guitar, and by the age of nineteen he could be found in nightclubs and concerts performing the songs of Bob Dylan, Leonard Cohen, and Simon and Garfunkel. He tried his hand at songwriting but without success.

Mistry emigrated to Toronto, Canada, in 1975 – coincidentally only a month after Indira Gandhi declared a state of emergency in India. He has frequently told reviewers that in order to become a success, a person of his age had to leave India. He says, *"There was more opportunity abroad."* (Mazzocco)

When he first arrived in Toronto Mistry worked at a bank, making use of the mathematics and economics degree that he had earned at the University of Bombay. Finding his position at the bank unsatisfying, he began to take English classes at York University, later moving to the University of Toronto to pursue a part-time degree in English and philosophy. He completed this second degree in 1982.

With his wife's encouragement, he tried his hand at story writing and soon won a short-story contest at the University of Toronto. He entered and won the same contest again the next year, and his work was anthologized in **The New Press Anthology of Best Canadian Short Fiction.** Penguin Books Canada published his first collection of stories in 1983, only three years after he had begun writing.

Mistry received a grant from the Canada Council in 1984. This money allowed him to quit his job at the bank and devote himself to writing full-time. In 1991, he came out with his first novel, **Such a Long Journey,** and won widespread recognition and acclaim. The novel was subsequently made into a film by the same name, directed by Sturla Gunnarsson. (Awards are listed below.)

A Fine Balance, published in 1995, won the Giller Prize, one of Canada's most prestigious literary awards. The novel also won the Los Angeles Times Book Prize in Fiction, the Commonwealth Writers Prize, and was short-listed for the Booker Prize. While the awards are wonderful, Mistry received a different kind of accolade – and a fabulous financial reward – when Oprah Winfrey declared **A Fine Balance** a selection for her hugely popular Book Club. The book's sales skyrocketed and Winfrey made Mistry a household name across Canada and the United States. Winfrey declared that **A Fine Balance** *"does what I believe a book is supposed to do. It transports you and opens you to new world experiences."* (Jain)

His book was selected shortly after Jonathan Franzen refused to have his book stamped with Oprah's seal of approval. Having never been bothered by Oprah's logo, Mistry was delighted to have his book selected for her club. *"I have no qualms about that because I am well acquainted with logos, having had so many on my books in the past – the Governor-General's, the Giller Prize, the Booker Prize short-list."* (Jain)

Mistry has commented on his attention to detail:

> *People have gotten used to reading more minimalist stuff ... So when they read something like this, with this level of detail, they assume it must be nonfiction. It's amazing how easily we get trained by the conventions of our time.* (Mazzocco)

Mistry on the anti-Hollywood conclusion of his novel:

> *Given the parameters of my characters' lives, given who they are, how can you expect them to have any more happiness than they have found? I think that the ending is a hopeful one: The human spark is not extinguished. They continue to find humour in their lives. This is an outstanding victory in their case.* (Mazzocco)

Mistry began writing **A Fine Balance** with a single image in mind:

> *It started with the image of a woman at a sewing machine. He initially planned to write a shorter novel, but he found it growing as he worked on it: "It seemed to be working as I wrote so I began letting the canvas grow ... I quickly realized that if I continued in this way, it was going to give me a unique chance to tell not just a story set in the city, but also a story about village life. India still lives in its villages (about 70-75 per cent of the population is rural) so this had a particular appeal for me."* (Shaikh)

Works by Rohinton Mistry

Novels

Family Matters, 2002 (winner of the Kiriyama Prize; short-listed for the Man Booker Prize)

A Fine Balance, 1995 (winner of the Giller Prize)

Such a Long Journey, 1991 (winner of Canada's Governor-General's Award, the Commonwealth Writers Prize, and the SmithBooks/Books in Canada First Novel Award; short-listed for the Booker Prize and the Trillium Award)

Short Story Collection

Tales from Firozsha Baag (also published as Swimming Lessons and Other Stories from Firozsha Baag), 1987

Historical Information

- Mistry's first novel, Such a Long Journey, is set in Bombay in 1971. The political backdrop of that novel is India's third war with Pakistan over the creation of Bangladesh, formerly East Pakistan. For his second novel, Mistry took up the next pivotal chapter of India's history. A Fine Balance is set in 1975, after Indira Gandhi's government has declared a state of internal emergency and has suspended numerous constitutional rights.

- India had been a British colony for hundreds of years, but in 1946, after Indian nationalists had long pushed for a sovereign state, British officials decided they would grant India independence if its leaders could agree upon a form of government. The New Congress Party and the Muslim League could not agree, and violence between Muslims and Hindus erupted throughout the country.

- Indian and British officials agreed upon a solution to the bloody quarrel: they would partition India into two separate nations – India and Pakistan. Sadly, this did not put an end to the bloodshed, and many people had to leave their homes: Sikhs and Hindus in Pakistan moved to India, and Muslims in India moved to Pakistan. The Hindu-Muslim riots serve as the backdrop to Ishvar and Om's story in **A Fine Balance.**

- On August 15th, 1947, the day after Pakistan achieved independence, India became an independent nation. Jawaharlal Nehru served as the newly independent state's first prime minister. His inaugural speech, delivered at the stroke of midnight on the 15th of August, 1947, pointed to India's long history of ups and downs.

> *At the dawn of history India started on her unending quest, and trackless centuries are filled with her striving and the grandeur of her successes and her failures. Through good and ill fortune alike she has never lost sight of that quest or forgotten the ideals which gave her strength. We end today a period of ill fortune and India discovers herself again.*

It seemed India itself would have to strike a fine balance between ill and good fortune.

- Nehru was generally considered a successful leader, leading the nation through a peaceful period. After he died on May 27, 1964, Lal Bahadur Shastri came to power. Shastri's rule was more violent and bloody than Nehru's had been: he declared war on Pakistan after it invaded two regions of India. Shastri died suddenly in 1966, after only twenty months as prime minister. He was succeeded by

Indira Gandhi, Jawaharlal Nehru's only daughter. Indira Gandhi's appointment to the head of the ruling Congress Party was considered a compromise between the right and left wings of the party; however, right-wingers in the party continually questioned her leadership.

• Shortly after her New Congress Party won a landslide victory in the 1972 election, her opponents in the Socialist Party alleged that she had committed electoral malpractice. In June 1975 the high court ruled against her, which should have meant that she would lose her seat and be obliged to stay out of politics for six years.

• To evade the consequences of the judicial decision, Gandhi declared an internal state of emergency on June 25, 1975. She imprisoned her political foes, passed laws that limited personal freedoms and placed the nation's press under strict censorship. Her son, Sanjay Gandhi, whom she was grooming as her successor, implemented large-scale forced sterilization as a form of birth control and ordered the removal of slum dwellings.

• When she felt certain that she had effectively quelled her political opposition, Gandhi finally called for open elections in 1977. However, she misjudged her support, and she and her party were defeated. She left office, but only for three years. She returned to Parliament in November 1978. As her son Sanjay was killed in a plane crash in 1980, Gandhi began to groom her second son, Rajiv, for the leadership of the New Congress Party. Gandhi ruled as prime minister again from 1980 until her assassination in 1984.

• In the early 1980s, several of India's different populations sought more independence from the central government. Sikh extremists in the Punjab region resorted to violence to advance their demands for autonomy. Gandhi responded by ordering an army attack on the Sikhs' holiest shrine, the Golden Temple of Amritsar, in June 1984. More than four hundred and fifty Sikhs were killed in this attack. In November 1984 Gandhi was assassinated in her own garden by two of her Sikh bodyguards.

- Indira Gandhi served as prime minister of India for three consecutive terms from 1966 to 1977, and again from 1980 to 1984. Under her leadership, India's democracy suffered immensely. Besides abusing the use of emergency measures, Ghandi also increased the use of military force in the nation, and she fostered a culture of nepotism. Her son Rajiv was sworn in as India's prime minister upon her death. Unfortunately, he too was killed, in his case by a suicide bomber during an election campaign.

- In May of 2004 Sonia Gandhi, Rajiv's widow and leader of the Congress Party, won the right to form a new coalition government and to make history as India's first non-Indian-born leader. Although widely popular and deemed a positive influence for the stability of the country, Mrs. Gandhi declined the opportunity to become prime minister, perhaps out of fear for her personal safety. **(Regg Cohn)**

CHARACTERIZATION

Dina Dalal

Maneck

Ishvar, Om

Others

CHARACTERIZATION

A Fine Balance takes us deep into the lives of four people whose daily life is a constant struggle – a struggle for food, shelter, and warmth. Mistry has commented on the four central characters in **A Fine Balance:** *"I don't think these people have been represented enough in fiction ... Most fiction is about the middle class; perhaps because most writers are from the middle class."* (Mazzocco) In trying to correct a too-common omission in fiction, Mistry uses this novel as a vehicle to showcase the lives of the poor and to bear witness to the will to survive in times of distress.

Main Characters: Dina Dalal, Ishvar and Omprakash Darji, Maneck Kohlah.

Other characters include Ibrahim, the rent-collector; Dina's brother, Nusswan, and his wife, Ruby; Shankar, the beggar; Rajaram, the hair collector; Monkey Man; and Beggarmaster.

Dina Dalal

- Dina has lived in the same apartment since her husband's death, never altering a thing. She is fixed in a moment of time, much like Dickens' Miss Havisham in **Great Expectations**. Like Miss Havisham, Dina has initial difficulty dealing with the reality of her loss. Unlike Miss Havisham, Dina is brought back into the bosom of society through her association with Maneck and the tailors. She knows that the road to survival does not lie in the past, so she *"seldom indulge[s] in looking back at her life with regret or bitterness."* (p.15)

- Dina loses her father to illness and then her husband to a traffic accident. When widowed, her mother had sunk into herself and virtually disappeared, but Dina fights her brother, Nusswan, in an effort to keep her independence and identity. *"Everywhere there was evidence of her struggle to stay ahead of squalor, to mitigate with neatness and order the shabbiness of poverty."* (p.230) She struggles to make the best of her impoverished surroundings, controlling her physical environment when she can control nothing else.

- Within the boundaries of India's layered society of rank and caste, Dina shows how barriers must be overcome in an effort to create a society that will benefit everyone. She fights with her own prejudices about Ishvar and Om and wins. Her struggle is to find *"the line between compassion and foolishness, kindness and weakness."* (p.445)

- Her independent spirit in this patriarchal society mirrors that of Indira Ghandi, who rose to become leader of India. Where Dina is kind and compassionate, Ghandi is cruel and politically selfish. (see Role of Women, p.35)

- Dina and Nusswan's relationship represents a constant struggle for control and has been strained since childhood. When Dina begins to mature, Nusswan's attention adopts a sinister edge – he seems intrigued by her body. Mistry does not linger on the incest angle in their relationship, since it's really only there for a moment.

- As Dina's eyes begin to fail her, she is suddenly more able to see the true natures of those around her. This is an old device in literature – the blind can always see more clearly.

Maneck Kohlah

- Maneck parallels Dina in terms of social class. They are both from the middle-class world, where they received a good education, had economic comfort, and an acceptable social status. Although their environments differ, their social standing provides much common ground.

- Maneck is a young student who has come from his home to study the profession of Refrigeration and Air Conditioning. He is the country mouse who has come to Dina's city. He hadn't wanted to leave his home or his family, because he envisioned himself as continuing in the tradition of his father and becoming the owner and manager of a retail business. Distraught and overwhelmed, Maneck exhibits Dukhi's concern about departing from a problematic environment. *"How can I leave that earth? It's not good to go too far from your native village. Then you forget who you are."* (p.124)

- Maneck's youthful acceptance of people and his naive innocence allow him to bridge the boundary between Dina's social level and the tailors'. He becomes great friends with Omprakash and gets to know him as someone with a personal history, rather than as an employee with a task to do.

- Maneck has the means, the intelligence, and the ability to overcome the obstacles in his life, but he is the one character who fails to survive. The very innocence and naiveté that enable him to see the world through another's eyes finally defeat him. Perhaps the layers of protection given him by both his parents throughout his life have left him without the strength and fortitude to deal with life's hurdles. Instead of letting the train of life carry him to the end of his track, Maneck throws himself onto the track prematurely.

Ishvar and Omprakash Darji

- Ishvar, the uncle, and Om, the nephew, come from the opposite end of the social spectrum to Dina and Maneck. If looked at only in terms of their caste, the reader might miss the strong personal ambition that Ishvar's father, Dukhi, had for his children. Also easy to miss would be the keen intelligence of Om's father, Narayan, and the fierce dedication of Ishvar's mother, Roopa, to her children. These are the common human characteristics that supersede social and economic standing, and Mistry portrays them beautifully.

- Through Ishvar and Om, Mistry shows how the unfortunate and downtrodden do much to care for those even less fortunate than themselves. These two men and their families represent the potential in human understanding and compassion for others, and the need to link arms and move forward. Ishvar, the elder, guides Om, the younger; sometimes it's the other way around. Together and in turn, they care for Shankar, the beggar, and Rajaram, giving of themselves even when they have nothing to give.

- The lovely intertwined relationship of these two men contrasts the behavior of the politically and financially established people, including Gandhi herself, who clearly promote their own interests at the cost of others.

- Uncle and nephew balance themselves both physically and in personality. *"Ishvar Darji was not a stout man; it was the contrast with Omprakash's skinny limbs that gave rise to their little jokes about his size."* (p.3)

- Ishvar is the essence of patience. He has experienced some of life's dangers, such as being gored by a bull, and is prepared to accept whatever life may present. On the other hand, Om is a typically impatient teenager who wants to face life head on. In fact, it is his foolish, hasty behavior that brings down Thakur's wrath and leads to a series of events that changes the balance of their lives forever.

- Ishvar's facial injury has forced his face to forever bear the reminder of necessary balance; he wears the masks of both tragedy and comedy at the same time. The humor that Ishvar and Om bring into many of their relationships, especially with Dina and Maneck, helps them to overcome life's daily challenges.

- Mistry contrasts Ishvar and Om with the other humorless characters whose economic and social standing isolate them from the nasty goings-on experienced by the general population. In that category, we find Dina's brother, Nusswan; Mrs. Gupta, Dina's supplier; and at the very top, Indira Gandhi, who has put so many barriers between herself and her people that she can't possibly know what they are living through. Mistry uses the tiers of the caste system as symbols of these layers of insulation; the further one gets from the bottom of society, the less one is capable of imagining them as equal human beings. (see Chess, p.55)

The Rest of the 'Caste' *In Alphabetical Order*

A host of characters darts in and out of the action of the story. This multitude of characters is a microcosm of the overcrowded population of Indian society

ASHRAF AND MUMTAZ CHACHI are Muslims, who take in the boys, Narayan and Ishvar, and train them as tailors. They are very kind and treat the boys better than the Hindu community from which they come. They are repaid in like kindness when the boys save them from being beaten or killed at the hands of a Hindu mob.

AVINASH, the student militant and Maneck's first friend in college, shows Maneck the possibility of another world. With his chessboard, Avinash tries symbolically to teach Maneck about the power and dynamics of politics. Unfortunately, both Avinash and Maneck are checkmated by their own and others' actions.

BEGGARMASTER is a walking contradiction in terms. He is simultaneously the oppressor and the savior of the poor and homeless. He makes his money through extortion and protection, and he is too often the one who creates beggars where there were none. He takes Monkey-man's niece and nephew, blinds them and cuts off their arms, thus creating for himself a new source of income. But he is equally capable of protecting his clientele. When he discovers that Shankar is his half-brother, he gives him extra-special treatment. He also protects Dina from her landlord, thus allowing her to enjoy extra time with her tailors and Maneck while pursuing her career.

DUKHI AND ROOPA are the parents of Narayan and Ishvar. Although they are born of the Chaamar caste, Dukhi especially has a sense of justice that exceeds his birthright. He believes that men should all be equal and wants his boys to rise above their status. He sends them to Ashraf, the Muslim tailor, to learn the trade of tailoring. Roopa, like many mothers, just wants to give her children the best that she can. She steals out into the night to find food and other things for her boys. She pays a price, however, with her body.

MRS. GUPTA, the owner and CEO of the Au Revoir Dress Company, is the capitalist who prospers in a socialist setting. By taking advantage of the government's state of emergency, she is able to pay low wages but makes a good living for herself – good enough to go to the hairdresser on a regular basis. Dina does not earn enough to treat herself in the same manner. Like Nusswan, Mrs. Gupta is the voice of the wealthier class, who supports Indira Gandhi. Because she doesn't see the humanity of the people below her, she can rely on the empty, but logically balanced, rhetoric of Gandhi's corrupt government to justify her own actions in business.

IBRAHIM, the rent collector, is another complex character with contradictions in both his personality and his actions. He finds himself uncomfortable in the mean-spirited profession he has chosen; he must throw people out of their homes onto the street. He harasses Dina, but in the final moment, morally exhausted by the tensions between them, he comes to warn her of the landlord's intentions. This act allows her to preserve her hard-won dignity. She moves out on her own terms.

THE KOHLAHS, Maneck's parents, represent the unchanging old guard, the intelligent middle-class, who prospered under the structure of the British occupation but who cannot cope with the changes brought about by Independence. Maneck, a child of the Independence era, feels stifled and isolated by the rigidity of his parents' outlook, especially his father's. His father's eye injury partially blinds him to the reality of a new India.

MONKEY-MAN is a human symbol for the balance of life when it is tipped. He loses his emotional equilibrium when his beloved monkeys are killed by his favorite dog. He fulfills a prophecy made at the time that life will offer him a worse tragedy and he will commit a horrible deed. He loses his niece and nephew to Beggarmaster, whom he later kills. The prophecy indicates that a single random act can set into motion a series of catastrophic events that may not be possible to avoid.

NUSSWAN is the overbearing brother who causes Dina much grief while she is growing up. Nevertheless, he always does his duty by his sister and especially comes through with a home and protection for her when she loses her flat and her income. **RUBY,** Nusswan's wife, is kind to Dina but silently agrees with Nusswan as to Dina's status in the household and uses her as a live-in servant.

RAJARAM, the hair collector, keeps disappearing from the story and recreates himself each time he reappears. He is a hair collector, a barber, a Family Planning Motivator, and lastly, Bal Baba, the holy man. After frequently borrowing money from Ishvar and Om, he finally happens upon the key to economic success – preying on the superstitions of the poor and uneducated.

SHANKAR is the armless and legless beggar, who rides life at ground level on a wheeled platform. His physical stature and his economic status put him, literally, at the bottom of the human ladder. But his inherent kindness to others at the work camp and on the street shows him to be head and shoulders above his oppressors in terms of human dignity and compassion. His is the only justice: he is given a funeral usually accorded to those in the upper castes

THAKUR DHARAMSI, a common thug, is the man directly responsible for the deaths of Narayan and his family, and for the castration of Om. This last assertion of power, cruel beyond all description, comes after Om and Ishvar have been forcibly sterilized.

VASANTRO VALMIK, the lawyer, is Mistry in cameo appearance. He is the calm, intelligent observer of the human behavior around him, and, most importantly, he is the advocate and recorder who intervenes on behalf of the unfortunates around him. He utters the central sentence of the novel, *"You have to maintain a fine balance between hope and despair."* (p.268) This sentence offers Mistry's main message, that life is not truly empty as long as hope is on the same table as despair. Like Rajaram, Valmik is a beneficiary of the fickle finger of fate. While Ishvar and Om are physically destroyed by the random events and sequences of their lives, and Maneck is emotionally destroyed by his lack of hope, it is Valmik's patience and acceptance of what life has to offer that is finally rewarded: he runs Rajaram's mail order business.

ZENOBIA, friend to Dina and Mrs. Kohlah, provides the link between Dina and Maneck and between Dina and Mrs. Gupta. Zenobia, like Mrs. Gupta and, to a certain extent, Dina, is a woman of independent financial means. This is another interesting pointer to the role and identity of women under Gandhi's matriarchal leadership. **(see The Role of Women, p.35)**

FOCUS POINTS AND THEMES

Caste System and Boundaries

Role of Women

Balance

Recycling

FOCUS POINTS AND THEMES

Indira Gandhi [was] a brilliant person, a good leader, who did a lot of good for the country. But I think when The Emergency was declared, she had become frustrated by the obstacles presented by this slow and messy and tedious process of democracy. We have to admit that democracy is messy. But it's the only way, or you see what happens. ... The villain is injustice. And that's the villain anywhere in the world where there is discontent and suffering. (Oprah) (see Historical Information, p.14)

The Caste System *Boundaries*

- Pandit Lalluram, the unofficial leader in Ishvar's village, tells Ishvar's father that *"there are four varnas in society: Brahmin, Kshatriya, Vaishya, and Shudra. Each of us belongs to one of these four varnas, and they cannot mix."* (p.130)

- According to traditional Hindu beliefs, the Brahmins are philosophers and priests. Originally, they did not work but were supported by the community because they performed various rites and offered spiritual and intellectual leadership. The Kshatriyas are the warrior caste, including kings and rulers, who protect the state. The Vaishyas are traders, involved in agricultural and mercantile affairs. The lowest caste, the Shudras, are laborers and perform menial services for the community. They are also known as "untouchables," and the other castes are not permitted to mingle with them.

- Through Dukhi and his friends, we are told the horror stories of how the untouchables are treated at the hands of their upper-caste bosses. There is a *"full catalogue of the real and imaginary crimes a low-caste person could commit ... [for the untouchable there is an] invisible line of caste he could never cross ... [he would need this knowledge] to survive in the village like his ancestors, with humiliation and forbearance as his constant companions."* (p.111) As we learn the details of their lives, we grow to understand and appreciate the immensity of each character's acceptance and forbearance.

- At the beginning, even Dina buys into the idea of class difference. In her attempt to keep Maneck and Om apart, she pleads that *"there is a difference, and you cannot pretend there isn't – their community, their background."* (p.341) This difference melts away later in the story when they realize that they have shared values.

- India's constitution, effective since November 1949, permits equality and justice to all its citizens. Today, however, many lower-caste people still have limited access to education and employment opportunities and are still performing the same menial tasks their fathers performed. This is especially true in the villages, although, as Mistry's novel indicates, life in the cities allows for more interaction, crossing of boundaries, and fluidity.

The Role of Women

- In India, past and present, the status of women has been paradoxical: there is the worship of Hindu goddesses juxtaposed to the burning of wives, the murder of female offspring, and the general rape and abuse of women. Although he doesn't deal directly with the violence against women, Mistry's attention to the women of the novel may have originated out of a concern regarding the power of men over women. There are subtle hints and references throughout the text. One example is the sexual extortion of Roopa when she seeks food for her children; another is the underlying hints of Nusswan's sexual attitude toward Dina and his attempts at domination by marrying her off to a prospect of his choice. A third example is the complete dependence of Dina's mother on her husband and subsequent inability to cope with life after his death; and finally there are the references to female infanticide in the lives of the lower and untouchable castes.

- Nevertheless, the women in this novel are generally strong, self-sufficient, and self-sacrificing characters. Ishvar's grandmother fasts when there is not enough food to feed her whole family. She foregoes what she needs so that her husband and children can eat. (p.111) Similarly, Ishvar's mother, Roopa, steals out in the night to take milk and fruit from others' property. She risks her own life to sustain and nourish her child.

- At the same time, women are noticeably mistreated in this society: *"special ardour and devotion... was reserved for male children"* (p.111) and female children are often even killed.

  > *The birth of daughters often brought them [the mothers] beatings from their husbands and their husbands' families. Sometimes they were ordered to discreetly get rid of the newborn. Then they had no choice but to strangle the infant with her swaddling clothes, poison her, or let her starve to death.* (p.114)

- What Mistry is exploring is the future possibility of a family-like structure where both genders are equally responsible for the happiness of those within its boundary. This is seen at its best in Dina's flat, where the four share companionship as well as the duties of shopping, cooking, and cleaning. This "family," which crosses caste and class lines, is linked emotionally rather than through bloodlines. Dina is happier with Ishvar, Om, and Maneck than she ever could be with Nusswan, Ruby, and their boys. However, in the end, she loses her independence and is forced to return to Nusswan's patrimony. The future has not yet arrived.

- As Mistry relates, *"I will say that if people can see in the book the importance of family, the human need for family – and by family I don't mean blood relations, I mean people – that is what redeems everything, ultimately... [M]any big stretches will reduce the amount of injustice in the world. There's no other way than making the big stretch."* (Oprah)

Balance

The fine balance of life is simultaneously a theme and a symbol. As a theme, balance is about equalizing and offsetting the opportunities and the struggles of life. As a symbol, the idea of balance represents the array of complex emotional, physical, economic, social, and geographic issues that everyone must face in life. Throughout their trials and tribulations, Mistry's characters hope that the good will outweigh the bad or, at the very least, there will be a harmony of good and bad. Consequently, many of the novel's characters spend a great deal of time evaluating and considering the idea of justice and fairness. They also spend a great deal of time suffering the imbalance of justice and fairness in their lives.

> *What sense did the world make? Where was God, the*
> *Bloody Fool? Did He have no sense of fair and unfair?*
> *Couldn't he read a simple balance sheet?* (p.690)

- One of Mistry's observations is that India, like the lives of many in her population, is at best a balance of contradictions. A good example of such a contradictory balance is Ibrahim, the rent collector. While his job is to be *"the landlord's spy, blackmailer, deliverer of threats, and all-round harasser of tenants ..."* (p.99), his inner thoughts reveal another side to him:

  > *... what ... had [he] done to deserve a life so stale, so*
  > *empty of hope ... Did the Master of the Universe take*
  > *no interest in levelling the scales – was there no such*
  > *thing as a fair measure?* (p.100)

- In his own small way he is sympathetic to Dina's plight and most of the time does not have the courage to enforce his threats. However, he does eventually bring the landlord's *goondas* in to forcibly evict Dina. But again, he contradicts himself by giving her fair warning.

At times, there is a breakdown and shift in the landscape of people's relationships. Their boundaries and values change and need to be rebalanced.

- An example of a new type of balance is explored through Maneck's family history. His family suffered a huge loss of property at the time of India's Independence in 1947. Like the arbitrary caste lines, India and Pakistan were divided up in a similarly random manner. It was a time when

  > *... two nations incarnated out of one. A foreigner drew*
  > *a magic line on a map and called it the new border; it*
  > *became a river of blood upon the earth. And the*
  > *orchards, fields, factories, business, all on the wrong*
  > *side of that line, vanished with a wave of the pale con-*
  > *juror's wand.* (p.236)

- Another example of an attempt to balance or shift certain defining boundaries is the caste system itself. We see Dukhi's desire for a better life for his sons, Ishvar and Narayan. Instead of raising them to be leather tanners as directed by their caste, Dukhi challenges the system and sends the boys to Ashraf to be apprenticed as tailors.

   > *What the ages had put together, Dukhi had dared to break asunder; he had turned cobblers into tailors, distorting society's timeless balance. Crossing the line of caste had to be punished with the utmost severity, said the Thakur.* (p.171)

- Dukhi was hunted and killed along with the majority of his family for daring to move the boundaries that demarcated his life. But as Dukhi shifts these boundaries to advance his family's fortunes, old prejudices die hard. When Narayan returns to the village and sets up a tailoring business, a Bhunghi, a person even lower than an untouchable, tries to have a garment made by Narayan. Roopa is outraged and expresses the same attitudes toward the Bunghi as Thakur Dharams had exhibited toward her family. *"My son does not sew for your kind!"* (p.153)

- It is interesting to note the humanistic values held by each of the novel's main characters and to see how these values are reflected in their behavior. The lower their status in life, the more humanitarian their values appear. The higher their status, the more distorted these values become. Gandhi, at the top, is shown to demonstrate the ultimate cruelty of a warped value system.

- Having boundaries and clearly marked lines of division helps to make order out of chaos, but boundary lines are soon shifted even in Dina's flat.

- o When Maneck moves in, he takes over Dina's bedroom, while she sleeps in the living room.

- o Dina tries to impose the boundaries of order with the tailors by first not allowing them to eat and drink from her dishes.

- o This changes when she permits them to keep their things in her flat.

- o The tailors subdivide the flat further when they finally assume residence on the verandah. Dina adds a final border when she awaits Om and his bride.

- Mistry uses these examples to show that boundaries between individuals and within class systems and political situations can never remain static and unmovable. Life is fluid and lines of separation are constantly blurred; these shifts can forever alter the balance of one's life. *"Places can change people."* (p.181)

A central thought in the novel is that the key to harmony and fulfillment in life is to find a balance between hope and despair. Mistry does not argue for a fifty-fifty share, but like the shifting boundaries of political partition and social caste levels, hope and despair also change their balance from time to time. When hope sinks, despair rises; when hope rises, it squelches despair.

- As the lawyer, Vasantro Valmik says to Dina, *"The secret of survival [is] to balance hope and despair, to embrace change."* (p.511) In the absence of a workable balance, there can exist a great lack of purpose and a feeling of insignificance.

- Dina experiences such a void when the tailors leave her house at the end of the day, and *"... the emptiness of her own life appear[s] starkest."* (p.224) This image of emptiness recurs repeatedly for Dina. Maneck experiences a similar feeling in Dubai, where the alluring promise of making money turns out to be an empty promise, as empty as the desert that surrounds the city. By leaving Dina's flat for Dubai, he enters a physical and emotional void.

- At the end of the novel, it is Dina who best illustrates the principle of filling a void by rebalancing her purpose in life. Her seemingly empty days in Nusswan's home are filled with her secret care of Ishvar and Om. In return for her acts of kindness, she has a more sustainable friendship and companionship than her family can provide.

- But it is Maneck who loses his balance in the most pronounced way. When he sees what has happened to Ishvar and Om, he is trapped by his feelings of despair. *"The words raced uselessly inside his head, unable to find an exit ... his words of love and sorrow and hope remained muted like stones."* (p.705, 706) For Maneck, the only way to survive or rise above your life is to lose your mind or to commit suicide. *"The slate wiped clean. No more remembering, no more suffering."* (p.392) He is trapped by a painful emptiness and he surrenders himself to the void.

- Like Mistry's characters, India's populace is constantly fighting for hope against the imbalance created by the greed of a corrupt political and social elite. The outcome of this struggle is the rise of a tidal wave of despair. *"Prohibition police are everywhere, you bribe one and ten more show up for their share."* (p.41) The ultimate corruption of hope is represented by Gandhi's electioneering process. The voting procedure is manipulated by the poll attendant, who later marks the ballot for the candidate of the overseer's choice.

- No matter which way they turn, the novel's characters find it difficult to balance despair with hope, but remarkably they keep trying. Mistry celebrates the universality of their efforts and addresses the universality of our human condition by encouraging our continued fight against all obstacles – large or small – that come along.

Recycling

- What cannot be changed, shifted, or balanced can be reused. Everything in this novel is recycled and nothing goes to waste. Because the people are too poor to throw anything away, they make the best of anything they can find, such as scraps of fabric and even garbage. People fight for the debris left behind by travelers on the train rails.

   The tattered army retrieved paper, food scraps, plastic bags, bottle tops, broken glass, every precious bit jettisoned by the departing train. They tucked it away in their gunny sacks, then melted into the shadows of the station, to sort their collections and await the next train. (p.598)

- Dina salvages every scrap of leftover cloth and finds a new use for these shreds in her sanitary pads. When these grow too numerous, she sews them into a quilt that holds all their memories.

- Beggarmaster claims that his business is *"looking after human lives."* (p. 426) When people become damaged or broken, unable to fend for themselves or work as "productive" members of society, Beggarmaster finds new uses for them in the economic marketplace. He capitalizes on their infirmities and essentially turns them into commodities, but at the same time he actually gives them a new lease on life.

- This emphasis on recycling should make us, in North America, consider what we take for granted.

WRITING STYLE AND STRUCTURE

Language

Narration

Tone, Mood

Foreshadowing, Structure

WRITING STYLE AND STRUCTURE

Language

- In his epigraph, Mistry quotes Balzac who writes: *"... rest assured: this tragedy is not a fiction. All is true."* This statement speaks about the way fiction illuminates the essence of truth differently from nonfiction. Fiction is not limited by historical fact and therefore can enter the mind and heart of a character more deeply than can a historian. It can carry us into what Northrop Frye calls *"a kind of enclosed garden in which we can wander in a state of completely satisfied receptivity."* (Frye, p.28) We become immersed in a world not our own through the framework and the style of the storytelling. Mistry's story expresses for us the things about India and its life that we may not personally experience.

- Mistry peppers his story with Hindi vocabulary, yet we are offered no glossary; there is an expectation that we'll strive to understand. Mistry encourages us to open our minds to another culture and work on a different level of comprehension. Because his use and rhythm of language so closely reflects the society in which it is based, his story gains credibility.

Narration   *The Storyteller's Voice*

- Mistry makes dozens of references to the art of storytelling – how it observes people and collects their stories, how it sorts these stories into a cohesive unit and gives us the final version, the novel, for our appreciation and enjoyment. *"... To share the story redeems every-thing."* (p.701) (This philosophy is shared by such authors as Peter Carey, Philip Roth, Ian McEwan, just to mention a few.)

- Maneck, Ishvar, and Om begin their physical journey by train. When Maneck and the tailors arrive at Dina's flat, Dina suddenly feels as though she is *"about to embark on a long voyage."* (p.12) The prologue ends and Mistry lets the story begin.

- Storytelling is an ancient oral tradition, where stories are passed from generation to generation. Dina and Ishvar, the older genera-tion, often tell the stories of their lives to the younger generation, Maneck and Om.

- The idea of storytelling becomes a useful tool for living. By telling stories, both the teller and the listener can face emotionally difficult situations vicariously and can, perhaps, learn something in the process.

- Vasantro Valmik, the lawyer, paraphrases Mistry's favorite poet, Yeats, and summarizes Mistry's philosophy about life and writing.

*I would never let emotions stand in the way of my pro-
fessional duties. Mind you, I'm not saying a proofreader must be heartless. I'm not denying that I often felt
like weeping at what I read – stories of misery, caste
violence, government callousness, official arrogance,
police brutality. I'm certain many of us felt that way,
and an emotional outburst would be quite normal. But
too long a sacrifice can make a stone of the heart, as my
favourite poet has written.* (p.266)

- Overexposure to a despairing situation can deaden the capacity to feel anything. The story offers a buffer and allows the reader's emotions to move around safely.

Tone, Mood   *Acceptance, Humor, Irony*

Although Om voices pessimism on many occasions, an atmosphere of for-bearance (Ishvar's and others') pervades. With few exceptions, Mistry's characters are amazing in their ability to adapt to and accept their sur-roundings, though their patience and emotional stamina are constantly put to the test.

- When Nawaz finds Ishvar and Om an alternative home in an illegal settlement, they learn to endure the degrading atmosphere. When that home is leveled and Dina does not allow them space in her home, they find shelter in the doorway of the pharmacy like so many other unfortunate pavement-dwellers.

    *Within minutes, huddled bodies had laid claim to all
    the concrete. Pedestrians now adapted to the new
    topography, picking their way carefully through the
    field of arms and legs and faces.* (p.363)

- Even in the end, with their lives in ruin, Ishvar and Om continue to forge ahead, all the while maintaining a sense of humor about their situation, at times bordering on self-mockery. Regardless, it is this quality that defines them as human and keeps them sane in an insane world.

  > *"Don't forget the umbrella." [Dina] tucked it under Om's arm. "It was very useful last night," he said. "I hit a thief who tried to grab our coins." He raised the rope and hauled. Ishvar made a clacking-clucking sound with his tongue against the teeth, imitating a bullock-cart driver. His nephew pawed the ground and tossed his head ...*

  > *"Come on, my faithful," said Ishvar. "Lift your hoofs or I'll feed you a dose of opium." Chuckling, Om trotted away plumply. They quit clowning when they emerged into the street.*

  > *Dina shut the door, shaking her head. Those two made her laugh every day.* (p.712, 713)

- Other characters, like Maneck's father, also believe that *"life [is] still good."* (p.237) When he loses an eye in a soda explosion, he muses that now *"the ugliness of the world would now trouble him only half as much."* (p.239) It is this sense of humor and perspective that is shared also by Om, Ishvar, and Dina. Ishvar lives by his mother's philosophy that *"the human face has limited space ... if you fill your face with laughing, there will be no room for crying."* (p.512)

- This has significance when we consider Maneck. Laughter is the force that allows the other characters to continue on with their lives, while Maneck's spark for life is slowly extinguished with each painful obstacle.

Foreshadow

- Mistry uses foreshadowing, the technique of hinting about future events, in a very heavy-handed way. But instead of giving the story away, this foreshadowing increases the foreboding mood and tension – we know that something bad will happen, but we don't know what or when. We become like the citizens of the novel, always waiting for the proverbial shoe to drop.

- The foreshadowing begins in a seemingly innocent manner when Dina says to Rustom: *"Are you ever nervous about cycling in this traffic?"* (p.37) Rustom is killed in a traffic accident on the eve of their third wedding anniversary. The forewarning then continues with the constant references to accidents on the train tracks where the *"train was delayed ... some poor fellow dead on the tracks again."* (p.89)

- In Maneck's very first conversation with Avinash, we are set up for his eventual suicide. Maneck describes the reciprocal relationship of his father's house and the mountainside to which it is joined by cables. If either the mountainside or the house lets go, it will be bad for the house. *"Sounds like a house with suicidal tendencies."* (p.274)

- This idea parallels Maneck's own tenuous relationship with his father. As his father anticipates that Maneck will let go of his family, Maneck's father lets go of Maneck, first by sending him to boarding school and then to the city to study a trade. But these gestures, designed to free him, leave him without a foundation, without a connection to cling to, and he finally lets go of life.

    When the first compartment had entered the station, he stepped off the platform and onto the gleaming silver tracks. (p.710)

Writing Structure

Mistry's novel follows a fairly conventional linear structure. In the first sections of the book, he brings together four disparate characters and explores each of their personal histories in a separate chapter. From this point on, his story unfolds in a straightforward chronological fashion.

- Because of this linear structure, and because he weaves together so many seemingly unconnected characters and incidents, Mistry has been compared with the great novelists of the nineteenth century – Charles Dickens, Leo Tolstoy, and Anton Chekhov. His writing style seems more in line with the tradition established by these epic-novel writers than it does with many of his own contemporaries. Many contemporary novelists let their novels evolve in a more fragmented, nonlinear fashion.

- Like so many of Dickens's novels, **A Fine Balance** depicts a city's underworld, concentrating not on the middle classes but on the poor. As critic Jamie James points out, Mistry's novel also includes a *"large cast of unforgettable minor characters, grotesque and humorous."* It is that sense of vastness, intricacy, and dropped threads that reminds readers of Dickens. His depiction of human nature, of naive central characters who are manipulated and used by the more greedy elements in society, is also reminiscent of Dickens' image of man.

- Mistry has barely commented on his connection to nineteenth-century novelists: *"I'm not an expert in all this so if the critics think my writing is Dickensian or Tolstoyan I will thank them, and say I am flattered."* (Shaikh)

SYMBOLS

Balance

Sewing

Train Transport

Chess

SYMBOLS

For me telling the story and being true to your charac-
ters is more important than demonstrating your skill
with words, all your juggling acts, the high-wire acts,
the flying trapeze acts. **(Shaikh)**

Balance   *The Bicycle, The Children on the pole*

- Riding a bicycle requires a balance of physical strength and strong
  perceptive skills. In other words, the rider must keep the bicycle
  upright, balanced on a single thin line of tire; the rider must notice
  the obstacles around him and be able to see far enough ahead to
  guide the bicycle through the obstacles to his final destination. What
  a wonderful metaphor for life! The only bicycle riders we encounter
  in the novel are Rustom and Om. *"Om on the saddle perform[s] an*
  intricate dance, the dance of balancing-at-slow-speed" **(p.216)**, while
  Rustom loses his balance and dies.

- When monkey-man ties the two small children to a fifteen-foot pole and lifts them into the night, balanced on his thumb, the balance of the audience's emotions shifts from entertainment to terror. An equilibrium has been broken, just as it is in life when danger becomes too close and personal. (p.420)

- Metaphorically, the balancing acts carried out by both the monkey man and the bicycle riders represent the precarious nature of life and refer to life's random sense of justice.

Sewing

- Sewing is closely related to the idea of recycling. Using needles and threads, Dina is able to reuse pieces of clothing to make piecework; in this way, nothing goes to waste. Dina, Maneck, Ishvar, and Om sew together a family from their disparate lives. As the different pieces of these characters' lives are made to fit together, some degree of adjustment is needed from each member of the new found family. And it is here that the metaphor of tailoring becomes significant. As the old adage goes, "The tailor makes the man"; similarly, the different characters give shape to their own lives to make them more suitable to their new positions.

  A lifetime had to be crafted, just like anything else ... it had to be moulded and beaten and burnished in order to get the most out of it. (p.48)

Train Transportation

- Trains provide movement between village and city. When the trains do not move, everything halts – there is no progress in the country. The train will be delayed when a person kills himself by jumping in front of it. Ironically, it is only during Indira Gandhi's emergency that the trains ran according to schedule. It is not necessarily the fault of the emergency that people commit suicide on the train tracks, but in a broader sense it is: as the economy declines, people turn to more drastic measures to relieve their pain. *"... yet another body had been found by the tracks."* (p.6)

- The body is a metaphor for the country, and the train tracks are like the veins in the body. Their proper functioning can signal the potential for freedom, escape, and a meaningful life. Conversely, there is also the potential for death.

Chess

- The use of chess as another metaphor for life fits on several levels. The chessmen are divided in function, pyramid-style, like the structure of a society. At the top are the king and queen, who are protected and insulated by the various layers of defense below them: rooks, bishops, knights. The major and most dispensable layer of defense consists of the identical pawns. Because they have no individual identities, these pawns are easily expendable. India's pawns are the poor, the homeless, the untouchables, all of whom exist at the bottom of the social pyramid.

- Avinash tries to use chess to teach the naive country boy, Maneck, about life. But all Maneck can see is that everyone's life is *"under a serious check ... Everything was under threat, and so complicated. The game was pitiless. The carnage upon the chessboard of life left wounded human beings in its wake ... Life seemed so hopeless, with nothing but misery for everyone."* (p.316) This is true for Avinash, his sisters, Dina, the tailors, Maneck's parents, and eventually for Maneck himself.

LAST THOUGHTS

LAST THOUGHTS

A Fine Balance

As is evident from the title of the novel, one of Mistry's primary themes is the idea of maintaining a precarious balance between all of the components of one's life. Mistry is a realist; he does not believe in black-or-white solutions. One must accept both the negatives and positives in life and piece them together in a way that does not compromise one's principles. Only then is it possible to reach for happiness.

- One of the novel's storylines discusses Maneck's coming of age. He is an idealistic young man who soon discovers that often life is not given to happy endings. Some readers may find the novel depressing and cynical because so many of the hopes and expectations of the characters are dashed.

- Yet in the end, Dina and her family scrape together what is left of their lives and find a degree of happiness. This, for Mistry, is a realistic portrayal of life. For example, when Dina is not satisfied with a part of her quilt, Ishvar tells her that,

  Calling one piece sad is meaningless. See, it is connected to a happy piece ... So that's the rule to remember, the whole quilt is more important than any single square. (p.568)

- At another place, the proofreader says,

  You cannot draw lines and compartments, and refuse to budge beyond them. Sometimes you have to use your failures as stepping-stones to success. You have to maintain a fine balance between hope and despair... In the end, it's all a question of balance. (p.268)

- The overarching theme of **A Fine Balance** can be viewed in many different ways. For one, Mistry frequently describes the country as a decaying body. This metaphor bears a relationship to the concept of a fine balance. The country, lacking the balance that every healthy organism should have, is decaying, rotting away. Injustice is the disease of the political body and misery, poverty, and hopelessness its symptoms; it is a disease aggravated by the isolation of parts that ought to work together.

FROM THE NOVEL

Quotes

FROM THE NOVEL

Memorable Quotes from the Text of
A Fine Balance

PAGE 15. Dina Dalal seldom indulged in looking back at her life with regret or bitterness, or questioning why things had turned out the way they had, cheating her of the bright future everyone had predicted for her when she was in school, when her name was still Dina Shroff. And if she did sink into one of these rare moods, she quickly swam out of it. What was the point of repeating the story over and over, she asked herself – it always ended the same way; whichever corridor she took, she wound up in the same room.

PAGE 100. Twenty-four years of drudgery and deprivation during which his youth disappeared, and the bright ambition of his golden season became tainted by bitterness. Desperate, and scarred by the certain knowledge that he no longer had any prospects, he watched his wife, two sons, and two daughters still believing in him and thereby increasing his anguish. He asked himself what it was he had done to deserve a life so stale, so empty of hope. Or was this the way all humans were meant to feel? Did the Master of the Universe take no interest in levelling the scales – was there no such thing as a fair measure?

PAGE 111. Thus Dukhi listened every evening to his father relate the unembellished facts about events in the village. During his childhood years, he mastered a full catalogue of the real and imaginary crimes a low-caste person could commit, and the corresponding punishments were engraved upon his memory. By the time he entered his teens, he had acquired all the knowledge he would need to perceive that invisible line of caste he could never cross, to survive in the village like his ancestors, with humiliation and forbearance as his constant companions.

PAGE 114. The news of a second son created envy in upper-caste homes where marriages had also taken place around the time Dukhi and Roopa were wed, but where women were still childless or awaiting a male issue. It was hard for them not to be resentful – the birth of daughters often brought them beatings from their husbands and their husbands' families. Sometimes they were ordered to discreetly get rid of the newborn.

PAGE 115. When the rumours started to spread, Dukhi feared for his family's safety. As a precaution, he went out of his way to be obsequious. Every time he saw high-caste persons on the road, he prostrated abjectly, but at a safe distance – so he couldn't be accused of contaminating them with his shadow. His moustache was shaved off even though its length and shape had conformed to caste rules, its tips humbly drooping downwards unlike proud upper-caste moustaches that flourished skywards. ... Whatever task Dukhi was ordered to do, he did without questioning, without thought of payment, keeping his eyes averted from the high-caste face and fixed safely on the feet. He knew that the least annoyance someone felt towards him could be fanned into flames to devour his family.

PAGE 142, 143. But the stories kept multiplying: someone had been knifed in the bazaar in town; a sadhu hacked to death at the bus station; a settlement razed to the ground. The tension spread through the entire district. And it was all believable because it resembled exactly what people had been seeing in newspapers for the past few days: reports about arson and riots in large towns and cities; about mayhem and massacre on all sides; about the vast and terrible exchange of populations that had commenced across the new border.

PAGE 316. Evening deepened the shadows in the room, but Maneck did not bother with the light. His whimsical thoughts about chess suddenly acquired a dark, depressing hue in the dusk. Everything was under threat, and so complicated. The game was pitiless. The carnage upon the chessboard of life left wounded human beings in its wake. Avinash's father with tuberculosis, his three sisters waiting for their dowries, Dina Aunty struggling to survive her misfortunes, Daddy crushed and brokenhearted while Mummy pretended he was going to be his strong, smiling self again, and their son would return after a year of college, start bottling Kohlah's Cola in the cellar, and their lives would be full of hope and happiness once more, like the time before he was sent away to boarding school. But pretending only worked in the world of childhood, things would never be the same again. Life seemed so hopeless, with nothing but misery for everyone.

PAGE 441. Splotches of pale moonlight revealed an endless stretch of patchwork shacks, the sordid quiltings of plastic and cardboard and paper and sackcloth, like scabs and blisters creeping in a dermatological nightmare across the rotting body of the metropolis. When the moon was blotted by clouds, the slum disappeared from sight. The stench continued to vouch for its presence.

PAGE 445. Morning light did not bring answers to the questions Dina had wrestled with all night. She could not risk losing the tailors again. But how firm to stand, how much to bend? Where was the line between compassion and foolishness, kindness and weakness? And that was from her position. From theirs, it might be a line between mercy and cruelty, consideration and callousness. She could draw it on this side, but they might see it on that side.

PAGE 637. Could she describe for Zenobia the extent to which Maneck and Om had become inseparable, and how Ishvar regarded both like his own sons? That the four of them cooked together and ate together, shared the cleaning and washing and shopping and laughing and worrying? That they cared about her, and gave her more respect than she had received from some of her own relatives? That she had, during these last few months, known what was a family?

PAGE 644. Where humans were concerned, the only emotion that made sense was wonder, at their ability to endure; and sorrow, for the hopelessness of it all. And maybe Maneck was right, everything did end badly.

PAGE 689. The photograph dragged Maneck's eyes back to it, to the event that was at once unsettling, pitiful, and maddening in its crystalline stillness. The three sisters looked disappointed, he thought, as though they had expected something more out of hanging, something more out of death, and then discovered that death was all there was. He found himself admiring their courage. What strength it must have taken, he thought, to unwind those saris from their bodies, to tie the knots around their necks. Or perhaps it had been easy, once the act acquired the beauty of logic and the weight of sensibleness.

ACKNOWLEDGEMENTS

ACKNOWLEDGEMENTS

Frye, Northrop. "The critical Path, an essay on the social Context of Literary Criticism." Toronto: Fitzhenry & Whiteside Ltd., 1971.

"Gandhi." Manas. *History and Politics.* http://www.sscnet.ucla.edu/southasia/History/Independent/Indire.html.

"Gandhi, Indira." *The New Encyclopedia Britannica.* Micropaedia. Vol. 5. 15th ed. Chicago: Encyclopedia Britannica Inc., 2002.

"Independence and Partition." http://www.linkup.au.com.india.

Hunt, Nigel. Review of A Fine Balance. *eye* magazine. http://www.eye.net/ye/issue.

Jain, Ajit. "Rohinton Mistry's book makes it to Oprah Winfrey's Book Club." rediff.com.http://www.rediff.com/us/2001.

James, Jamie. "The Toronto Circle." Atlantic Online. http://www.theatlantic.com/issues/2000.

Mazzocco, Mary. "Rohinton Mistry became an author almost by chance." Knight-Ridder Newspapers. http://lubbockonline.com/news.

Oprah's Book Club. "A Fine Balance Discussion." http://www.oprah.com.

Nuzeh, Christina. "Meet the Writer: Rohinton Mistry."
Barnes&Noble.com. http://www.barnesandnoble.com/writers

Regg Cohen, Martin. "Gandhi 'humbly' Bows Out." *Toronto Star*, May
19, 2004.

Ruddy, Martin. "Rohinton Mistry." National Library of Canada.
http://www.nlc-bnc.ca.

Shaikh, Nermeen. "Q & A: AsiaSource interview." AsiaSource.
http://www.asia source.org/news.